Willie
the Whale

First published in 2002 by
Franklin Watts
96 Leonard Street
London
EC2A 4XD

Franklin Watts Australia
56 O'Riordan Street
Alexandria
NSW 2015

A CIP catalogue record for this book is available
from the British Library.

ISBN 0 7496 4477 X (hbk)
ISBN 0 7496 4623 3 (pbk)

Series Editor: Louise John
Series Advisor: Dr Barrie Wade
Cover Design: Jason Anscomb
Design: Peter Scoulding

Printed in Hong Kong

Willie the Whale

by Joy Oades and Barbara Vagnozzi

W
FRANKLIN WATTS
LONDON•SYDNEY

Willie the Whale
woke early one day
and told all his friends
he was going away...

...to swim to the North,
to the South, East and West,

and maybe to stay

in the place he liked best.

Willie's first stop was
at the South Pole.

8

He swam under the ice
and popped up through a hole.

9

A seal and a penguin

were startled to see

Willie the Whale

on his round-the-world spree.

He didn't stay long,

though it looked very nice.

"I'll never get used
to the snow and the ice.
While the seals and penguins
are happy and free,
it's far too cold
for a fellow like me."

New York was next
on Willie's tour list.
It was certainly somewhere
not to be missed.

With buildings so tall,

right up to the sky,

even Willie felt small

as he slowly swam by.

He saw all the sights
but found it too busy.
It made Willie Whale
feel really quite dizzy.

"It's nice here," he thought,
"and the statue is pretty.
But there's no room for a whale
in this crowded city."

17

He swam on his way
till he came to a land
where all he could see
was the sun and the sand.

A humpy old camel
had such a surprise
when Willie appeared
in front of his eyes.

Willie basked in the sun
and he thought for a while,
then he swam down the river
that they call the Nile.

20

"The desert's all right
for a sun-loving camel,
but it's a little too hot
for a sea-loving mammal!"

21

Great London town
seemed very inviting.
The parks were so pretty,
the people exciting.

Willie thought to himself,
"It's the best place I've seen –
I'll go to the palace
and visit the Queen."

But, alas for poor Willie,
a sightseeing spree
is not for a whale –
he's too big, you see.

25

And how can a whale
walk down the Strand?

A whale must have water –
it can't live on land!

So Willie set off
for the wide, open sea,
where the ocean is endless
and whales can swim free...

And he spouted and sang
as he cruised through the foam –

for, as everyone knows,

there's no place like home!

Hopscotch has been specially designed to fit the requirements of the National Literacy Strategy. It offers real books by top authors and illustrators for children developing their reading skills.

There are five other Hopscotch stories to choose from:

Marvin, the Blue Pig
Written by Karen Wallace, illustrated by Lisa Williams
Marvin is the only blue pig on the farm. He tries hard to make himself pink but nothing seems to work. Then, one day, his friend Esther gives him some advice...

Plip and Plop
Written by Penny Dolan, illustrated by Lisa Smith
Plip and Plop are two pesky pigeons that live in Sam's grandpa's garden. If anyone went out, Plip and Plop got busy... So Sam has to think of a way to get rid of them!

The Queen's Dragon
Written by Anne Cassidy, illustrated by Gwyneth Williamson
The Queen is fed up with her dragon, Harry. His wings are floppy and his fire has gone out! She decides to find a new one, but it's not quite as easy as she thinks...

Flora McQuack
Written by Penny Dolan, illustrated by Kay Widdowson
Flora McQuack finds a lost egg by the side of the loch and decides to hatch it. But when the egg cracks open, Flora is in for a surprise!

Naughty Nancy
Written by Anne Cassidy, illustrated by Desideria Guicciardini
Norman's little sister Nancy is the naughtiest girl he knows. When Mum goes out for the day, Norman tries hard to keep Nancy out of trouble, but things don't quite go according to plan!